RED JACKET

A PREQUEL TO SHADOW APOCALYPSE

THE DARKLE CHRONICLES
BOOK 0.5

B.C. HOLLYWOOD

Edited by Jonathan Butcher (Developmental)
Edited by Hannah Cole (Developmental)
Final Copy Edit by 360 Editing (a division of Uncomfortably Dark). Editor: Candace Nola.
Cover: Hollywood Imaging

ISBN 13: 978-1-0686757-0-6

WARNING

This book is an extreme apocalyptic fantasy-horror story. It contains graphic depictions of violence, reference to SA, and cannibalism. Reader discretion is advised.

DARKLE

Dar-kle

1. To appear darkly or indistinctly.

2.

a. To grow dark.

b. To become gloomy.

CHAPTER 1
LILLIAN

Lillian surveyed the valley from her vantage point on the hillside. A light haze diffused the early morning sunlight as occasional bird flight disturbed the air. In the valley below, the motorway snaked its way from town south-easterly towards the city, a grey slashing wound through the lush green. No vehicles travelled upon it, but their carcasses littered its length. It was impossible to believe that only a handful of years ago, the motorway bustled with the chaotic energy of rush-hour traffic as commuters hurried to work. *The end of the world was good for something,* she thought.

She caught movement on the opposite side of the valley and squinted against the sun. Tiny forms travelled toward Tara, too distant to discern much detail, but she recognised them. *A smoker and its herd.* The group was too large, and too boldly displaying themselves to be anything else. She shivered, thinking, *I'll never get used to those cold bastards.*

Behind her, the ruined church loomed. The weight of what lay within was an almost physical thing. She turned to confront it.

The old stones were roughhewn and weathered, a chaotic

mix of greys, whites, and blacks, with the occasional green, lending the ruin a sullen look. It had once been a church of some denomination or another, but nobody living knew which one or cared. As she moved into the archway, she imagined being swallowed whole.

———

Stepping from darkness into the sky-lit central area where the congregation once gathered, she followed a trodden pathway through the meadowed grass to where the altar once stood. Something had lain there too, creating a large rectangular flattening. A used condom hung in the stalks of grass to one side, dripping blackish blood and other fluids.

Crows scattered as she walked by, cawing their protest at the interruption and revealing the meal they feasted upon. A naked undead woman's corpse rested on a bed of smouldering clothing. The colour and general condition of her skin showed she had recently turned. Nothing remained of her milky eyes; the crows had seen to that. They'd punctured the smooth skin elsewhere, sharp beaks ripping her flesh. Another puncture wound at her temple gaped, raw and bloodless, administered by human hands. It had facilitated her final departure.

Lillian noted an empty bottle of whiskey close to the fire, and nearby, four evenly spaced indentations imprinted the ground. *A fucking garden chair?* The image formed of the miscreants warming themselves by the fire as they waited their turn with the walking corpse. Little else remained of the night's festivities.

Shaking with suppressed rage, she uncapped an old cola bottle and poured the piss-coloured liquid over the corpse. She stepped back as the embers took the fuel in a whoosh. As she watched the clothes ignite, she hoped it would be enough to take the body too. No thoughts or prayers occurred to her; the world was long past their usefulness.

————

Lillian returned to her vehicle in the small parking lot next to the crumbling ruins and the charred remains of a country pub. The arson had happened years ago, at the beginning of the end. The pub was just another ruin harkening back to a lost time.

Before she reached her vehicle, as she crossed a muddy spot close to the rusted entry-gate, a fresh tyre mark caught her attention. It was wide and sunk deep with weight. *A four-by-four,* she thought. *Another piece of the puzzle.* Four-by-fours weren't rare in those days of uncertainty, but she filed it away, nonetheless.

Leaving the mark to the elements, she got into her vehicle. The early start of the day had soured from the scene in the church ruins, but she might still rescue it. Her next stop was Burke's farm. The hint of a smile brushed the corner of her mouth as she thought of seeing Megan again. It had been too long.

CHAPTER 2
BURKE'S FARM

illian entered Burke's farm by way of the tree-lined, winding lane, walking to get a better feel for the defences. She went unchallenged.

They're so exposed, she thought, and vowed to warn Peter Burke again. Every time she visited with them to trade, it was the same, but maybe he would see reason this time.

The yard was a hive of activity and had a genuine small village feel, as though the farm existed in a pocket universe of some bygone day. She suspected the carefree atmosphere was responsible for the overall lax security.

A call of "Lillian!" from across the yard, and Megan came bounding into view. She was an awkward child, but her coordination had improved these past months.

"Hey, Megan," said Lillian.

Megan came to a skidding halt before her and got straight to the point. "Can we practice today?"

The twelve-year-old's enthusiasm was hard to resist, and Lillian wondered if she had ever been so passionate about something at that age. "You've been working on the targets?"

"Yep. I can almost hit the bullseye most of the time." Megan smiled shyly.

"Nice! Get your bow and I'll meet you behind the barn after I've spoken with Peter," said Lillian. She noticed Megan's face twist into a grimace at the mention of the farm owner. "Everything okay?"

"Yeah. He's been in a mood all day. Since those strangers called this morning," said Megan.

"Strangers?"

"Uh-huh. Three of them." Megan grimaced again. "They looked really mean. Peter has been like a wasp since they left."

"Any idea what they wanted?"

Megan looked shocked. "What would I know? Sure, I'm only a child."

Lillian raised an eyebrow and smiled faintly.

A moment of this was all Megan could stand before she cracked. "Okay! I might have overheard them talking. They said they wanted to trade. Weapons for as much food as we had. But Peter told them we had all the weapons we needed, and that other people relied on us for food too, so they couldn't have it all."

"How did they take that?" Lillian asked.

"The one doing all the talking smiled and shrugged. He looked meaner when he smiled. Peter should have got some weapons from them."

Lillian didn't respond to that. "Get your bow. I'll be with you in a while."

Megan gave a mock salute and said, "Yes, sir!" She bounded awkwardly away and didn't see the frown on Lillian's brow as she walked to the farmhouse.

———

"They sound like trouble, Peter," said Lillian. They were in the farmhouse kitchen and Lillian had her trade items arranged on the large oak table for Peter to view. So far, he'd chosen a small hand-axe, two bottles of painkillers, and a box of antibiotics.

"I'm not worried about them," he said, in the same dismissive way he always responded. "This is a safe place, Lillian. If the smokers stay away and the storm always passes us by, we have little to worry about from the likes of those."

Lillian pictured the last smoker she'd seen up close, an undead businesswoman, given purpose by the dark essence which had taken over. Then she pictured the unnatural cloud that roamed the countryside, consuming all before it and leaving only death in its wake. "You know there's a difference between people who are just plain bad, and either the smokers or that cloud. There are sick assholes out there who hunt down female undead and subject them to—." A flash of something at the farmhouse window made her pause. *That girl!* Grateful for the chance to compose herself, Lillian took a deep breath to suppress the hint of strain in her voice. Now wasn't the time to delve into that topic, but she made a mental note to ask Peter about any signs he may have seen later on.

She went on, "Your decisions affect more than you, Peter. They look to you for guidance, and if you're not careful, you'll get these people killed." Lillian knew by the grim set to his mouth that she'd gone too far, but she didn't care. He needed to hear the truth.

Peter said nothing, just selected two rolls of tape and a random selection of candy bars, pulling them into his pile of items. "Thank you for your concern, but we're safe here. You can collect your produce outside. See you next week." And with that, he turned and left.

Lillian shrugged. *There's no talking to fools,* she thought. Peter was right about the smokers, and therefore most of the undead, avoiding the area surrounding the farmhouse. And the nightmare cloud had never gotten within a mile of the place. She didn't know why that was, and if Peter did, he wasn't telling her. Ancient sites and odd shaped mounds surrounded the area, which, for all she knew, could have once been sacred places. She hoped the effect worked on evil of the more human kind, but she doubted it.

She'd been on the lookout for the zombie-fuckers for months but had no success in finding them; they moved around randomly and Lillian had only picked up occasional signs of their passing. That morning was the first sign they were back in the area in weeks. But this new group of assholes was more worrying; they seemed organised. *Who has enough weapons to trade with anymore?*

———

"Nicely done!" said Lillian.

Megan beamed at the praise as she went to fetch the arrows. Lillian watched as the gangly girl ran down the field to where three makeshift targets were propped against a stack of hay bales. Megan's aim had improved exponentially over the past months. When they'd begun training, she was lucky if she hit a target once out of three shots. Today, she hadn't missed once, and each hit had been like a surgical strike.

Megan was still smiling when she strolled back to Lillian.

"You're almost as good as me now," said Lillian.

"You think I'm ready for live targets?"

Lillian nodded. "For sure. I'll come early next time, and we'll go hunting—"

"Yes!"

"For rabbits! Let's start you on something small."

The size of their prospective prey did not dampen Megan's enthusiasm. *And why would it? All parts of a rabbit are useful*, thought Lillian. "It's late. I've got to head out if I'm to make it home before dark."

"Aww," said Megan.

"Don't forget to take care of that bow like I showed you. And store it properly afterwards."

"Yes, sir!" And another salute.

"Less of the 'sir', you cheeky sod!"

Lillian turned back towards the yard, leaving the girl to tidy up the practice area. She'd collect her produce and the trade gear Peter didn't want. She didn't expect to see the man again that day, and that was okay with her. There'd been enough arguments already. *I'll try talking sense into him in a few days.*

CHAPTER 3
THE EVIL EYE

A few days later, Lillian approached the farmhouse with caution, staying low and using the surrounding cover to conceal herself. Light pouring from the downstairs window pierced the early morning darkness. The drone from the generator in the attached shed filled the air.

Apart from the house lights, there was no sign of life. Lillian inched closer, her breath held, as she moved towards the nearest window. She froze as a deep, masculine voice broke the silence, originating from somewhere on the other side of the house.

"Come on ta fuck," he said.

A younger man's voice responded from inside, closer to her. "Calm down. I'm near done."

The man at the front spat out a string of expletives, clearly dissatisfied, which elicited a chuckle from the youngster within.

Lillian eased her knife from its sheath.

From the front came the slam of a vehicle's door and the roar of an engine starting. The lad inside exclaimed, "Fuck!" replacing his previous mirth.

Lillian used the loud engine noise to mask her rush to the farmhouse wall. She peered through the window.

A young, ginger-headed youth, wearing a worn leather jacket covered in heavy-metal patches, dropped a can of paint, and took off toward the front door. The spilled blue paint mixed with the splashes of red already on the floor.

When the young lad reached the front, Lillian heard him call, "Hold on, ya cunt!"

"Took yer sweet time for a bit of paintin'."

"Ye can't rush art."

The vehicle door opened. "Art me hole. Are you sure you weren't riding one of them?"

"Fuck off!"

The vehicle door slammed, and the engine roared as it sped off.

Lillian relaxed, but she took a deep breath to steady herself before reaching for the back door.

———

A slaughterhouse greeted Lillian as she stepped inside. The door opened directly into the spacious farmhouse kitchen and all around it lay twisted bodies. An eerie silence enveloped the room, only disturbed by the muffled hum of the generator.

A quick look around revealed the familiar faces of the farm's residents. Individual flashes of extreme violence assailed her: bloodied, broken limbs; exposed flesh, sliced and beaten and abused.

She shut her eyes against them to regain her concentration. *Breathe.* Opened them again with a level head.

Some bodies were incomplete. Their limbs twisted at unnatural angles, with bones protruding through torn flesh. On others, bruises, cuts, and burns covered every inch of visible skin, creating a grotesque tapestry of pain. The stench of blood and decay hung heavy in the air, mingling with the palpable aura of fear and despair. Flies gathered.

On a bed made of their tattered clothes, some lay naked, their bloodied orifices agape from rough handling, their tear-streaked faces unmoving beneath glazed eyes. Peter's wife, Maggie, his daughter Kath, and a quiet girl who always greeted her with a shy smile. *What was her name?*

Lillian's heart sank as she realised the extent of the horrors endured by these poor souls. Tears welled up in her eyes, blurring her vision as she fought to maintain composure. Each incomplete body served as a haunting reminder of lives brutally cut short, leaving behind a trail of unanswered questions and shattered dreams.

Violence had woven itself into her life, starting with her past as a victim and continuing as she became the perpetrator. But the level of suffering inflicted in the kitchen tested even her limits. She tried to push through the overwhelming anguish, forcing herself to examine the scene with a clinical eye. The sheer violence inflicted upon the farm's residents made it difficult to ascertain the exact number of victims. Bodies were strewn across the blood-soaked ground, dismembered parts scattered. *Such savagery!*

Lillian's hands trembled as she reached out to touch one of the disfigured bodies, her fingertips tracing the jagged edges of a deep laceration. The physical evidence of the unspeakable acts committed against these individuals was a harsh reminder of the evil that existed in the world. It was a reminder that justice needed to be served, and those responsible for this heinous crime needed to be held accountable.

Taking a deep breath, Lillian steadied herself, determined to find answers amidst the horror. She moved among them, lifting and turning as she searched for one in particular, hoping against hope she wouldn't find her. Then she spotted Megan's familiar braids beneath the large oak kitchen table. *No!*

Lillian rushed over and found the girl, twisted and discarded. She pulled her limp form into her arms, checking for signs of life, but abandoned her efforts after a few minutes. There was no pulse and not a whisper of breath.

Megan's body was still warm, so she couldn't have been dead long. "Fuck!" *If I had gotten here sooner.*

As Lillian checked Megan for the fatal injury, sorrow overwhelmed her, but her mood turned cold when she saw the blood trails on the inside of Megan's upper thighs. *Bastards!* She wished the violation of a young girl surprised her, but personal experience taught her otherwise. And that was before the world had turned to shit. The assault hadn't killed Megan, though she probably wished it had. Blunt force trauma to the back of her head had ended her life.

Lillian gently lay Megan's body back on the floor and brushed a lock of hair from her face. She looked so peaceful, as though sleeping. On impulse, Lillian used her knife to remove a lock of the girl's hair, as a keepsake, and pocketed it.

She stood and glanced over the scene. Her heart ached at the absence of survivors. The once busy surroundings now bore witness to a nightmarish tableau.

Peter lay crumpled in one corner, close to where his family had been raped. He looked relatively unmarked, apart from the dark blossom of red on his chest from a gunshot wound. "You got off lightly," said Lillian. *Maybe I can remedy that.* She grabbed his feet and dragged him out of the kitchen and into the farmyard. Leaving him at the water-pump, she retrieved a roll of bailing twine from the ransacked storage area and used it to tie his feet to the pump. Stepping back, she said, "You're a fool, Peter. I'll deal with you later." *If you get up again.* She hoped he was one of those who did.

Lillian entered the kitchen again and took in the ginger youth's artwork. He'd painted the symbol of an eye, a menacing and ominous emblem, on the empty interior wall. It loomed large over the scene, casting a foreboding shadow on the room. Painted in icy blue, it stood as a chilling reminder of those responsible for what unfolded here. Its piercing gaze seemed to follow Lillian around, instilling a sense of unease in her. On closer inspection, the intricate details of the symbol sent shivers down her spine, depicting a malevolent eye surrounded by twisted, serpentine tendrils, an apt calling-card for the monsters behind this atrocity. And they were monsters, as far as Lillian was concerned. No-one with an ounce of humanity could do what she saw there. The evil eye was a macabre signature left behind by these merciless fiends. The knowledge that the evil eye could strike again at any moment would haunt anyone who saw it.

Lillian gritted her teeth as she stepped over the bodies, her gait shifting to that of a prowling animal. *We'll see about that.*

CHAPTER 4
THE CULT

Lillian used the rickety wooden steps to climb into the loft of Burke's barn. She found the long metal box along the wall, away from the grimy window. An old bed sheet obscured it from prying eyes, but Megan had entrusted her with the box's location and the hiding place of a spare key. She'd wanted to know if it was a good enough spot.

Inside the box lay Megan's compound bow, alongside a quiver of arrows. Another pack of arrows lay at the back, on top of which sat a small container with dry cloths and wax. Megan had ensured the bow was clean and had freshly waxed the string. She'd done a good job.

Lillian retrieved the weapon and took the braid of Megan's hair from her pocket. She wrapped it around the bottom limb and tied it securely. Lillian hefted the bow and felt satisfied. *I'll make sure you see some blood,* she promised.

Lastly, she took the quiver of arrows from the metal box and looped them around her neck. She tucked the spare arrows under her arm before heading for the generator room beside the farmhouse. The raiders had cleared the room of fuel cans, leaving only the empties, but she siphoned what remained in the generator into a small can.

Inside the farmhouse, she poured the fuel over the bodies and broke up what furniture she could gather from the rest of the house in the kitchen, covering them.

Satisfied with the makeshift pyre, she exited to the yard and struck a match to ignite a piece of card.

"None of you deserved this, but I promise I'll avenge you." She threw the card through the door and waited. After a few moments, smoke began to rise, then flames licked the windows, and the curtains caught with a whoosh. She had to step back as the heat intensified, but she watched on, despite knowing how unsafe the blaze she set would be; who knows what the flames might draw.

Lillian imagined the feeling of the inferno on her skin was the call of those within for vengeance. It fortified her resolve.

———

With the farmhouse ablaze behind her, Lillian set to tracking the raiders. She'd retrieved her own vehicle and picked up the tyre marks of the raiders' truck easily enough. She'd heard them drive away in a northeasterly direction that morning, so she headed that way, keeping her eyes peeled. *They can't have gotten far*, she thought.

The road by the farmhouse was a minor one, and the hedges had encroached over the past years through lack of traffic, so the passing of a truck left its mark, but she had to take it slow when she approached each junction to watch for changes in direction. The more distance she covered, the slower she went; she didn't want to speed into the back of them. Surprise was the one thing she had going for her.

By her side, on the passenger seat, lay Megan's bow. Each time she looked at it, it gave her encouragement that the path she had chosen was worthwhile.

As she drove, she considered the raiders. She inferred that the two men were part of a larger group based on the chaos inflicted upon the farmhouse residents. If that was the case, they may not have ranged far. Moving larger groups was logistically complicated. So, once she'd travelled ten kilometres without sighting them, she took to stopping every half kilometre to shut off the engine and listen. It further slowed her pace but was worth it when she heard the distant sounds of screaming from further up the road.

Hopping into her vehicle, she reversed it until she found a wide gateway where she could pull off the road. She grabbed the bow and quiver and proceeded towards the noise on foot.

———

Keeping to the field side of the hedgerow that ran along the road, Lillian approached the raider encampment. An assortment of vehicles, from humble family saloons to campers and busses, along with trailers towed by some of them, formed a wide semicircular perimeter on each side of the road. She crept closer, using the meadow's tall grass as cover, so she could see within. Her initial impression was that they were much larger and better organised than she'd expected.

A sentry positioned twenty meters from her, on the roof of a camper, showed more interest in the goings on within the camp, where each new agonised scream elicited the sounds of people jeering and cheering. Lillian inched through the grass towards a four-by-four with plenty of room beneath. When the next scream broke the air, she dashed as the sentry craned his neck around for another look. Before the crowd finished jeering, she concealed herself in the shadows beneath the four-by-four.

From her vantage point beneath the four-by-four at the camp-side edge, she saw a haphazard arrangement of mismatched tents in her immediate vicinity. No people were moving around the tents in this area, but perhaps they made up the jeering crowd, although the sight of them remained obscured. *Fuck! I need to get closer.* It would be safer to skirt the edge of the camp, using the vehicles as cover, but the screaming was jarring her nerves. Under her breath, she muttered, "Fuck it!"

Lillian exited the shadows and stood. Slinging the bow over her back, she walked through the tents as though she belonged there. As she reached the edge of the tents, the source of the screaming and jeering became apparent. A mob, perhaps one hundred or more men and women of mixed ages, gathered around a raised platform standing between two colourful carnival tents. On the left end of the platform, two raiders held a screaming middle-aged woman and forced her to watch as another two raiders held a middle-aged man. He screamed in agony, but the raiders next to him blocked Lillian's line of sight. She moved to get a better view while keeping to the edge of the tent area, then un-shouldered the bow and positioned it alongside her leg to conceal it, but still have it at hand.

With her view unobscured, Lillian saw that the middle-aged man's left arm had been amputated at the elbow and someone had cauterised the wound using a brazier full of coals. A tendril of smoke snaked into the air from his stump and the man was barely conscious.

Towards the back of the raised area, a group of five men watched on. They wore black robes, were shaven-headed, and each had a blue mark on his forehead. Lillian couldn't make it out at the distance, but she'd be willing to bet they depicted the same blue eye from the farmhouse wall. *Crazy looking bastards,* she thought. In front of the five cloaked men, knelt three children of varying ages. A raider lifted the smallest, a girl of perhaps five, and led her away. The woman screamed again, hysterical in her intensity, and pleaded with the tattooed leaders on the stage.

Ignoring the woman, the one in the middle rose from his place and addressed the mutilated man. "Well done. You have saved your young daughter. Next your oldest child. You may free her for your right leg." The leader sat down again to observe the proceedings.

The oldest child, a boy of about ten, shouted, "Dad! No!" The woman crumpled in on herself and fell to the ground, sobbing. The mob roared its approval.

The mutilated man roused himself long enough to say, "Just fucking do it."

A nod from the now seated leader to the raiders attending to the father and one of them went to work applying a medical grade tourniquet on his right leg. Once in place, the second raider took a hacksaw from a bag that Lillian hadn't noticed.

Bending down, the raider began to saw through the man's leg. Initially, the denim put up a fight, but eventually yielded to the tenderness of the flesh underneath, blending the noises of torn fabric with that of cutting meat and bone. The man's screams pierced the air, clearly audible above the jeering mob, even as the blood and pain whipped them into a fervour. When the job was halfway done, the screaming stopped as the man, mercifully, passed out. The raider continued his grim task and eventually the leg hung down from the last fragment of skin and denim. Then it dropped to the stage with a flat slap. The crowd roared their appreciation, those closest to the stage drumming on it excitedly.

"Revive him," said the leader, not rising. "Or the game ends in a loss for him."

His emotionless, matter-of-fact voice sent a chill through Lillian.

The mother didn't react. She was too far gone into the solace of insanity, but the two remaining children broke free from their watchers and rushed to each other. They held each other for comfort, for the briefest moment, before the raiders tore them apart again.

A bucket of water was thrown onto the mutilated man and he regained consciousness, much to the mob's approval. The leader said, "Excellent. You have now freed two out of three children. Admirable." He instructed his followers to lead the older boy away, and they brought him to the same exit as the youngest girl.

The cloaked leader addressed the remaining child, a girl of seven or eight. "Your father has freed your siblings through brute determination. I admire him for that. But your life is now in his hands."

The leader smiled at the girl, and Lillian shivered. *There's no humanity there,* she thought.

The leader turned to address the girl's father. "One child left and all you have to do to save her is kill your wife." The volume of the mob rose to a new height, but the leader waved for silence. He turned to the woman. "But why should he have all the fun? You may kill your husband to save your child."

At that, they dragged the woman to her feet and brought her to her husband. They put a knife in her hand and she looked at it, not comprehending its purpose. They put a knife in the man's remaining hand too, but it fell out of his grip and onto the stage. To Lillian, the man looked like he was moments away from death.

The remaining child shook as she watched the nightmare scene unfold. Lillian ached with compassion for her. Seeing her in distress brought back some of Lillian's own childhood traumas. But she was impotent to act. What could one person do against so many? *What indeed...*

Before she could think about it too much, Lillian stepped away from the tents and into the open. She lifted the bow, pulled an arrow from the quiver at her side, and nocked it.

The raiders and mob encouraged the couple, while the council of assholes watched on, but she remained unnoticed.

"Hey, assholes!" Her shout rang out across the field and the mob turned as she drew the bow and let loose.

Time slowed, and the arrow seemed to hang in the air for an eternity, before everything happened at once. The arrow buried itself dead centre in the leader's forehead and the mob gasped.

Lillian shouted, "Bullseye!" Flipped the crowd with her middle finger, then turned and ran full tilt back through the tents, not waiting to see who followed. If the noise was anything to go by, the entire camp was in pursuit.

Sporadic gunfire sounded, so she kept low as she zig-zagged her way to the perimeter, where she slid under a school bus. She took a chance and ran through the meadow, still keeping low. No shouting or gunfire followed her until she'd reached her vehicle, when she heard a shot and a thunk of impact as she hopped into the driver's seat.

CHAPTER 5
PURSUIT

Lillian accelerated away from the gateway, leaving a cloud of dust and debris billowing across the road as she headed back toward the farmhouse. Moments later, just before a turn would obscure them, two vehicles burst through the dust-cloud. She prayed the drivers didn't know the roads as well as she did.

After a series of sharp bends, she hit a straight stretch and floored it. The engine protested as the torque pulled her back into the seat. The vehicle lurched forward. She glanced in the rear-view mirror as she neared the next junction, a crossroads, and saw the two pursuing vehicles racing to catch her. An unexpected thrill of excitement coursed through her.

Braking hard at the crossroads, she considered her options. Her racing heart pulsed at her temple, as her eyes shot left and right. *Keep your shit together and choose!* She floored the gas pedal and her car spun into a daring dance at the centre of the junction. The tyres gripped the tarmac, creating a symphony of screeches that reverberated through the still air.

As she executed the perfect doughnut, a cloud of dust rose, enveloping the intersection in a transient shroud.

Lillian's laughter echoed in harmony with the mechanical ballet she orchestrated, transcending the ordinary into a momentary spectacle of sheer audacity. Another loop, and the cloud widened and thickened. Because of her inability to see anything, except for the vague outline of what was the left-hand turn, she was certain that the approaching raiders couldn't see her either.

She tore away from the crossroads and viewed the scene in her rear-view. She marvelled at how the sunlight filtered through the suspended particles and cast a surreal glow on the mundane junction, just before a dip in the road brought it out of sight.

———

The rear end of Lillian's car protruded from the hedge at a sharp corner of the narrow road. Lillian viewed the scene critically from concealment on the opposite side. *They'll see right through it, if they even come this way*, she thought, but readied herself should her pursuers chose the correct route.

The engine was still running, and the seatbelt warning *binged* in time with the flashing hazards. She hoped the combination of lights and engine-noise wasn't too much. *Maybe I should have killed the engine.* It was too late to do anything but wait, however.

From the direction she'd come, she heard the distant buzz of an engine growing louder. She hunkered down further and notched an arrow to her bow. Her heart pounded against her chest, the adrenaline coursing through her veins. The tension in her muscles intensified, causing a slight tremor in her hands as she held the notched arrow. Beads of sweat formed on her forehead, despite the coolness of the surrounding air.

The distant buzz grew into a roaring engine, its sound echoing through the trees. Her senses sharpened; every sound amplified in her ears. She strained to distinguish any clues that might show how many vehicles approached. *If it's more than one, I'm fucked.* Her breaths came in shallow gasps, her body preparing for the imminent encounter.

As the sound grew, her grip on the bow tightened and her knuckles turned white. That initial rush she experienced at taking out the maniac leader had faded, along with the adrenaline of the chase. Now fear mingled with determination within her, a cocktail of emotions. The weight of the situation pressed down upon her, but she refused to let it break her.

Whispering a silent prayer under her breath, her voice barely audible, she sought solace from a divine presence she wasn't sure existed. In this moment of uncertainty, she clung to the hope that some higher force would guide her through the impending danger. It was a desperate plea, born out of desperation and the need for protection.

As if to answer her prayer, the engine's sound became clear. *Just one!* The vehicle slowed as it approached her apparent accident. Before it stopped, the passenger side door swung open, and a rough-looking man jumped out. He pulled a business-like sawn-off from his belt and crouched low as he closed the distance to her car.

The back door swung open, revealing a young woman adorned in a white leather biker jacket and a snug matching skirt. "Is she there?"

"Shut the fuck up!" Sawn-off admonished without looking at her.

The driver remained in the car, keeping it running. Lillian couldn't see them, but she hoped they stayed put. She had enough to deal with…

Lillian rose to a kneeling position from her hiding place amidst the foliage, careful not to make any noise. Sawn-off reached the open driver's side door of her vehicle and peered in as she drew the arrow back.

"Bitch isn't here," said Sawn-off as he turned back to Biker-girl. His eyes widened as he caught sight of her loosing the arrow. "Fuck!" He pivoted, bringing the shotgun around, and fired a wild shot in her direction as the arrow struck his left shoulder. He cried out and dropped the firearm.

Off target, but I'll take it, thought Lillian. She moved to the left to use the tree there as cover, but stumbled on a protruding root. She tumbled onto the road where Biker-girl bore down, pulling her own weapon from beneath her jacket.

Lillian scrambled to get back up and just made it as Biker-girl reached her. Biker-girl's mouth twisted into a nasty smile as she aimed the small-calibre handgun at Lillian.

"What are you going to do now, bitch?" Biker-girl said, echoing Sawn-off.

Sweat trickled down Lillian's forehead as her body tensed up, a mixture of fear and anger coursing through her veins. Her heart pounded in her ears as her mind raced, desperately searching for a way out of the dire predicament. Thoughts of self-preservation and survival clashed with her natural instincts to fight back. *Think, damnit!*

Despite the fear that threatened to consume her, Lillian's determination burned bright. She knew she had to survive for vengeance's sake if no other. Every beat of her heart pushed her to fight back, to defy the odds stacked against her.

"I asked you a fucking question, bitch!" Biker-girl snarled.

At that moment, Lillian made a choice. She forced a smile and took a step forward, her eyes locked on Biker-girl's malevolent gaze. The world seemed to slow down as she reached for her knife. She was ready to face whatever came next with unwavering resolve. *I'll go down fighting!*

A shot rang out and Lillian flinched, but there was no pain. Biker-girl's eyes widened before she fell forward revealing another woman pointing a smoking gun where Biker-girl had been. Lillian reasoned the woman was the driver, but why she'd shot one of her own was anybody's guess.

"What the fuck, Emily?!" Sawn-off wasn't pleased. He

moved to gather the shotgun from the ground with his left arm, but he was clumsy.

The driver, Emily, seemed frozen in place. Lillian knew if someone didn't do something quickly, they were both fucked. She ran to Biker-girl and prized the peashooter from her grip as Sawn-off raised the shotgun and tried to aim. With a burst of energy, she rushed at him and pulled the trigger at near point-blank range.

Blam!

Sawn-off fell back on the road, dead but for some twitching.

———

Lillian turned to the woman, Emily, who still pointed her handgun to where Biker-girl had been. Her hand trembled. Lillian lowered the peashooter to her side and waited to see what the woman would do.

Emily wore a fire-engine red patent jacket and a tight black skirt that hovered over a pair of black fishnet stockings. *Where do these girls shop? Hookers-are-us?* Lillian suspected the dead meathead at her feet, or one like him, chose both their outfits.

"Your name is Emily?" Lillian asked in a calm voice, to which the woman responded with a slight nod. Before Lillian could thank her, Emily spoke.

"Curtis was a bastard and deserved it," she said, glancing at Sawn-off, "but Julie was okay, just a bit stupid."

There was desperation in Emily's eyes and her lips trembled as the enormity of her actions hit her. Lillian thought she could easily slip into hysteria. She'd need to be careful. "I'm sorry you had to stop her from killing me, but I'm glad you did, Emily. Thank you."

Another small nod. "You killed one of the Eyes," she said, a note of disbelief in her voice. She blinked and turned to look directly at Lillian for the first time as she lowered her gun. "Can you kill the others?"

"Tell me about them," said Lillian.

———

They talked as they worked, erasing all signs of the trap Lillian had set.

"I fell in with them a year ago and Curtis took me under his wing. Which meant he got to have me first and got to say who else could." Emily's eyes went distant, then took on a spooked expression. "Except for The Eyes, they take whatever they want."

Emily's exposed skin showed signs of bruising. Some were fresh, some almost healed. To Lillian's eyes, the woman hadn't had it easy. "What's their game? Another end of the world cult?" Lillian had seen a few of those. Preaching hell-fire, but only in it for control. Same old, same old, as far as she could see.

"Yeah. Some old god I'd never heard of until I met them. He has an evil eye; that's what the tattoos are about, and the name everyone calls them. You know. The Eyes."

Lillian grunted in acknowledgment as she bundled Curtis into her vehicle.

Emily continued. "But those guys really believe that shit. Say they're helping the old god bring about the end of days. Through pain and torture of anything that's remotely good."

"They sound like assholes," said Lillian.

"They are, but dangerous assholes. And most of the camp swallow their shit whole."

"But not you?"

"First chance I get and I'm out of there," said Emily.

"Why not leave now? Take the car and don't look back."

Emily shook her head without a second's hesitation.

"Nobody gets away. Not alive, anyway. Believe me, many have tried."

"So, you need to cut the head off the snake. Is that it?"

"Yes. When I saw that arrow take out The Eye, I felt a little hope."

"A little hope will get you killed," said Lillian.

————

A little later, they shared a cold meal within earshot of the now cleared accident site. No other raiders had turned up.

"Let me get this straight. You want me to go back to the camp with you and kill the rest of those maniacs with the tattoos on their foreheads?" Lillian asked. She wouldn't admit it to Emily, but that was more or less her intention. *Better she thinks it's her own idea.*

Emily didn't look the slightest bit embarrassed when she answered. "Yes."

"While pretending I'm your friend over there?" Lillian looked at Biker-girl's body where it lay alongside that of Curtis to one side of their hastily set up camp. They had parked both vehicles close by. Broken foliage and splashes of blood were the only signs of violence out on the road.

Emily looked at Biker-girl's body. "Believe me, nobody will notice the difference if you wear her clothes and copy her makeup." She looked Lillian up and down appraisingly. "The men won't see past your ass, and we can keep away from the other women."

"And Curtis? How do you explain him?"

"We can say you killed him?"

Lillian noted the uncertainty in Emily's voice, but let it go. Overall, it was a solid plan. "Okay. I think we can work with this."

————

There's a lot to be said for using the right tool for the job at hand, Lillian mused, as she whacked the top of the survival knife with the tyre-iron to drive the blade through Biker-girl's neck bone. It went halfway through but the next hit severed head from body. The cut was jagged and messy, but did the trick.

Lillian placed the tyre-iron and knife to one side and raised the severed head by the hair. She turned it from side to side, examining it. "What do you think?"

"It looks close enough to you. Julie's hair was about the same length and colour as yours. With her face cleaned like that, it's enough to fool a casual glance," said Emily.

They'd stripped Biker-girl first, so as not to destroy the clothes with gore, and Lillian had used a damp cloth to wipe what blood there had been on the white leather jacket and skirt from the original altercation. Lillian removed her own clothing and slipped on the stockings. Then she squeezed into the skirt. It just about fit, but she wouldn't be performing gymnastics in the outfit. The white leather biker jacket was better and at least offered some protection should they be attacked.

In the wing-mirror of her vehicle, Lillian copied Biker-girl's black eye makeup with campfire soot and engine oil. *Apocalypse-skank,* she thought. She was out of practice, with social appointments over the past few years being minimal. Tying her hair like Biker-girl's took seconds. When all was done, Emily nodded. "You'll pass."

"Yeah. Well, I'll stick with you. If anyone asks why I'm quiet, say I'm in shock over Curtis," said Lillian.

"Are we bringing him with us?" Emily looked at the corpse in distaste.

"Would they expect us to bring back his body?"

Emily shook her head without needing to think about it much. "No. They'd leave him where he fell. There'd be no more use for him dead."

"Okay. Bring my bow and arrows. It'll add authenticity."

Lillian hated the thought of handing over Megan's bow to those animals, but she couldn't keep them on her and would risk losing them altogether if she hid them in the countryside.

She placed the severed head, compound bow, and quiver of arrows in the back seat of the vehicle. The clothes were tight, and her legs felt cold and exposed, but the worst part was that the outfit reminded her of a life she'd long since left behind. She didn't like that one bit. But quitting wasn't an option. Quitting had crossed her mind whilst planning, but each time it occurred, she'd seen Megan lying in the farm-house kitchen and she'd gritted her teeth and pushed through. Besides Megan, she didn't think the family that The Eyes had been torturing when she interrupted had much time left, if any. "Come on," she said, "let's get this over with."

Emily was already in the driver's seat, so Lillian got into the passenger seat. Emily gunned the engine and took the vehicle back onto the road.

CHAPTER 6
INFILTRATION

They timed it so they arrived back at the camp as night fell. Thanks to the perimeter fires placed at regular intervals, as well as a larger bonfire at the centre, they could see the camp from a couple of miles out.

Emily took them straight to the main entrance, which followed the road that cut straight through the camp. A nod to the sentry was all it took; he recognised them. *Recognised Emily, anyway,* thought Lillian, keeping her face in shadow as well as she could.

The smell of cooking meat wafted in the cracked windows as soon as they passed the perimeter. Lillian's mouth watered. "What's cooking?"

"You don't want to know," said Emily.

Lillian caught Emily's flickering glance to the right of the road ahead and followed it. A group of people busied themselves around three cook-fires, over each of which a large pig was being turned on a spit. Lillian frowned. *What's wrong with the proportions?* She hadn't seen the entire camp, but there'd been no sign of livestock on her brief earlier visit. "Pigs?"

A tight shake of Emily's head.

Fuck! Thought Lillian as realisation dawned. *The children.*

She felt the bile rise from her stomach but fought it down. They were eating the children she'd seen being tortured earlier. "Is this because of me killing one of them?"

Another head shake from Emily. "No," from gritted teeth.

"You eat people?"

Emily was silent for a moment. "You eat enough so you won't be eaten."

Lillian made a low whistle. "That's pretty fucked up, Emily."

The woman did not try to disagree. She turned the vehicle left and pulled in beside a medium-sized tent. "We shared this with Curtis. You go in and I'll bring the head to The Eyes."

"I should go with you," said Lillian. She second guessed herself putting her trust in Emily. *Eating people?* Lillian had done some outlandish things, but she'd never resorted to eating human flesh. Aside from that, why wouldn't Emily just betray Lillian as soon as she got to The Eyes? Lillian fought to calm herself. *If she betrays me, she betrays herself. She put the bullet in Julie.*

"Best you stay here. Someone might see through the disguise," said Emily.

"It's a little late questioning the plan now, don't you think?"

Emily got out of the vehicle and retrieved the severed head, bow, and arrows from the back. "I won't be long."

Lillian nodded before getting out of the car herself and stomping over to the tent flap. She needed to put on a good show for whoever was watching. The hair at the back of her neck raised at the same time as she sensed someone watching her. She felt eyes burning into her and she was glad she kept the sawn-off shotgun belonging to Curtis. She felt even more glad that it was loaded.

———

Lillian paced the tent for an eternity, always only a pace or two from the primed weapon. She didn't dare keep the firearm in her hand because of the suspicion finding her that way would raise, but she itched for it.

She froze as footsteps approached and only released the breath she held when Emily entered. Emily looked troubled.

"What's wrong?" Lillian asked.

"They want to see you."

Lillian didn't need to ask who they were. "What happened?" She should have gone with Emily, but wasn't about to ruminate in hindsight.

"It's fine. I think. They bought the head being yours. The bow helped. But they want to thank you for your part in bringing vengeance down on… well, you."

"Why the worried face?"

The frown again. "They're used to getting whatever they want. So, if they want you, they'll take you."

Lillian understood. Emily was so used to the life she found herself in that she couldn't see an alternative. "Don't worry about me. When do they want to see me?"

"Now."

"Shit." Lillian looked at the shotgun. "I suppose that's out of the question."

Emily shook her head. "You'll never get it past their guards."

Lillian nodded and cast her eyes about for a concealable weapon.

Movement from outside the tent followed by a gruff voice. "What's taking so long?"

The whites of Emily's eyes showed as she answered, "Julie was sleeping. She's getting dressed."

"Hurry the fuck up!"

Voice low, Emily hissed, "Come on!"

Out of time, Lillian cursed under her breath and swiped up the only halfway serviceable item she could find. A metal nail file. She slipped it into the waistband of her skirt and indicated for Emily to lead the way. Exposed as the leather gear made her, having no proper weapon made her feel completely naked.

———

The walk through the camp to The Eyes' tent felt like an eternity to Lillian. People were up and about, drinking and making noise, in an atmosphere of forced festivities. On the surface, it was hard to believe that one of their leaders had been murdered only hours before, but if you looked a little deeper, you could see a frantic light behind people's eyes. *They're scared and shouting into the dark because of it,* she thought.

Before they were halfway to their destination, Lillian sensed being watched again, but given the pools of fitful firelight within a sea of darkness, it was impossible to locate the watcher. She glanced at Emily, but the woman did not indicate that she was any more uncomfortable than she'd been inside the tent a few moments ago.

They passed the three cooking fires from earlier, and Lillian noted the fires had been banked down. No meat roasted on the spits. She was about to whisper a question to Emily when a man who didn't look like a guard approached.

"Julie?"

"Fuck," said Emily in a whisper. She turned to the man, blocking his view of Lillian. "Not now, Trevor. We're heading to The Eyes."

Lillian turned her head in the opposite direction to hide her face.

"Everything alright?" Trevor asked.

"Yeah, everything is grand. We'll talk later," said Emily.

"Em, sure."

They hadn't stopped walking and must have crossed

some sort of boundary between the main camp and the area where The Eyes were because Trevor stopped walking and followed them the rest of the way with his eyes. *He knows,* thought Lillian. And why wouldn't he? She didn't know Julie and did not know how she carried herself. All she had was a set of clothing and a rudimentary likeness to work with. *This is such a bad idea,* she thought, but it was too late to turn back. *In for a penny, in for a pound.*

Two guards stood at the main tent opening, one to either side and both armed. One held a rifle in a relaxed manner, but at the ready. He looked comfortable and capable. The other had a couple of hand axes at his belt, mean-looking weapons that would cause mayhem in a fight.

The guard who guided them wore a brutal-looking survival knife on his belt, but he left it at the entrance before leading them in. As Lillian passed by, it seemed like the two guards ignored her, but her instincts told her they assessed and dismissed her. *Trained, but not that well trained.* She ducked her head and followed Emily and their escort in.

———

The interior of The Eyes' tent was spacious and luxurious. An impressive thirty feet across, it could have hosted a small circus. Coal braziers, placed at irregular intervals, offered fitful light, accented in a sickly yellow glow from a selection of oil lamps placed on low tables. The decor reminded Lillian of a hodgepodge mix of Germanic, Norse, and Roman commanders' tents, like something she'd seen in movie theatres when there were such things.

A raised area against the wall opposite the entrance was a clear focal point. Four out of the five throne-like seats had occupants. Lillian thought they were the same seats The Eyes had used outside on her earlier visit.

Two other guards seemed to languish to the sides, one at

each wall. Lillian didn't buy it; they looked alert and as capable as the ones guarding the entrance. They were unarmed, as far as Lillian could see. This meant either they were experts in hand-to-hand combat, or The Eyes were at least a little paranoid and didn't trust their own royal guard, so to speak. The first might be problematic, but the second would be a definite advantage. *Of course, both could be true,* she thought, but hoped that wasn't the case. Lillian noted they were big guys and hoped that meant they were slow.

Servants navigated through the many guests, who clustered in twos and threes, exchanging hushed conversations. Lillian smiled. Whispering and splintered groups spoke of internal strife.

Their guard took them past a table laden with food, at the centre of which sat the roasted meat from outside. A serving attendant busied herself carving up the largest of the roasts, the carving knife slicing off juicy slabs of meat. Lillian assumed it was the ten-year-old boy. Her stomach rumbled at the rich smell of the food, a cruel betrayal. A murmur of conversation permeated the air, and she saw more than a few hungry looks darting towards the banquet as tongues wetted lips.

On close inspection, Lillian couldn't mistake the source of the meat. The shape of the small human bodies was glaringly apparent. How the limbs connected to the torso and the proportions of those limbs to each other left no room for doubt. She swallowed back the urge to vomit and stared straight ahead. She focused instead on the raised area they approached and its occupants.

The one empty seat was on the left end, not in the centre where she had created the vacancy. This close, she noticed the centre seat stood higher than the two seats on either side. The outside seats were also lower than the other three. *Some sort of hierarchy then?* She suppressed a smile. *Did I cut off the head of the snake?*

Their guide stopped before the raised area and might as well have saluted. The new snake's head in the centre seat waved him away with barely a look, and the man didn't need to be told twice. He stepped back and Lillian heard him retreat at least a few paces. The man in the centre seat focused on Emily and Lillian.

"Hail, the conquering heroes," he said in a disingenuous drawl.

Emily lowered her gaze to the floor, so Lillian copied her, but in the moment before doing so she got the impression of a frail framed, sickly individual, more so than the other Eyes.

"In His name, Brother Nathan," said Emily.

"In His name, Brother Nathan," echoed Lillian. She hoped she was doing as expected but had no way of knowing. Her hand inched towards her waist and the secreted nail file.

"Yes, yes. In His name," said Nathan in a way that made Lillian think it was a scripted response, like the exchange made between priests and their congregations. "Tell us again how you avenged Brother Michael. Leave nothing out."

"Yes, Brother," said Emily. She cleared her throat slightly, but from what Lillian could see, watching from the corner of her eye, the woman didn't raise her gaze to look at any of the seated men. *What's that all about?* It struck Lillian as some backwards, repressive, patriarchal, cult-like behaviour, and she didn't like it one bit. Her hand was as close to the nail file as she could get it without making it obvious that she was up to something.

Emily continued. "Me, Curtis, and Julie split from the others after losing Brother Michael's killer at a crossroads. It wasn't long before we found her car at what looked like an accident - her car was in the ditch. Curtis and Julie had a look, but the bitch wasn't dead, and it wasn't no accident. She killed Curtis with that bow of hers." Emily raised her head and directed her look to the side where Lillian's bow and the quiver of arrows lay against a cushion upon which rested the real Julie's bloody head.

Thank Christ for that, thought Lillian. *If I can get to that bow...*

Emily cleared her throat again and went on. "Julie got the drop on her when she was distracted by Curtis. We took the weapon and her head for you."

"Why just the head?" Brother Nathan asked. He was quiet and intense, which lent weight to the question.

"Didn't think we needed more."

"Didn't think. Indeed. It doesn't look like it was easy separating it from her body."

Lillian didn't like where the conversation was going, but she couldn't speak up because she didn't know who in the room knew the real Julie.

"It was easy enough before we started," said Emily, then, almost an afterthought, "Brother."

From the other three seats, a chorus of chuckles. Lillian dared a flickering glance up at Brother Nathan and saw the rising fury in his face. *Careful, Emily.* Brother Nathan was too new to his position and the last thing they needed was to be made an example of.

Brother Nathan rose from his seat and approached them, stopping between them.

"What about you, Julie? Was that how it happened?"

It took a moment for Lillian to realise she was being addressed.

"Yes, Brother," she said.

Lillian froze as Brother Nathan reached out and placed his clammy fingertips beneath her chin. This close, she didn't think he'd notice her hand moving, so she edged it closer to her waistband. His hand felt weak as a day-old kitten, but she allowed it to raise her face upward, so their eyes met.

"Are you—" he said, then a glint of recognition. His eyes widened. "You!"

Moving quickly, Lillian grabbed Brother Nathan's hand in her left one and twisted it around. The surprise movement forced him to turn away from her and double over as she twisted his arm behind his back. An agonised cry escaped from him as she applied pressure, giving her time to retrieve the metal nail file from her waistband. Another moment to bring the small object around and she dragged the sharp hook at its tip across his eyes. They made dual, soft popping sounds before the blood and jelly flowed down his face.

CHAPTER 7
CHAOS

All hell broke loose in the tent as Lillian shoved Brother Nathan forward. He stumbled onto the front of the platform where he kneeled screaming, his hand scrabbling across his ruined eyes, fingers exploring the bloody sockets.

Beside Lillian, Emily stood in shock, wide-eyed and open-mouthed. Lillian pushed her towards Julie's head, shouting, "The bow!"

Emily almost stumbled but kept her feet. Lillian didn't wait to see if she got the weapon but whirled around. The languishing guards to either side had already sprung into action and were closing in on them, one on Emily and one on Lillian. She ignored them both and focused on the closest threat.

The guard who had brought them there was almost as dumbfounded as Emily and stood wide-eyed and mouth agape between Lillian and the banquet table. Keeping the advantage, Lillian charged at him and before he could gather his thoughts, she planted a devastating kick to the groin. He dropped to his knees and brought his hands down far too late to protect his manhood. Lillian used the opportunity to gouge out his carotid artery using the sharp tip of the metal file as she passed. Blood fountained out, but she'd already forgotten him.

The servant at the food table still gripped the sharp knife and long two-pronged fork as Lillian reached her, and for a moment Lillian thought she would fight, but something in Lillian's eyes dissuaded her. She dropped both implements to the banquet table, but the knife was at the edge and fell to the floor with a clatter. The servant ducked under the table and out of sight.

Lillian sensed the once languishing guard bear down upon her and she dived for the carving knife, swiping it up. Rising to her feet, she turned to face him. She brandished the knife, waving it back and forth between them in what she hoped was an amateurish way. The guard grinned at her show and loosened his shoulders to prepare for a fight. She didn't know if that meant he bought the ruse or not.

In the periphery of her vision, she saw the other guard reach Emily. *Just my luck to get the fast one*, she thought. Emily had retrieved the bow and arrows, but the proximity of the guard made it impossible to use them, if the woman even knew how. She was effectively helpless.

"What are you waiting for, bitch?" the guard facing her asked. Lillian's skin crawled. *I hate that word!* She wondered if, in the world before, guys like this practised being unpleasant in a secret asshole school. *The first rule about Asshole Club is don't talk about Asshole Club.* Should the opportunity presented itself, she swore she'd carve 'ASSHOLE' across his chest.

"What are you waiting for, bitch?" Lillian echoed, matching his intonation perfectly. It had the desired effect, and he lunged at her, but she sidestepped and slid onto and across the banquet table, kicking the smallest roast wildly in his direction. She picked up the two-pronged fork on the way.

Asshole corrected his direction and turned to face her,

easily avoiding the small child-roast. *Damn! He's fast!* She was glad of the table between them, and the extra weapon; she needed all the help she could get.

He was pissed and readied himself for the attack. Lillian prepared to meet him, but his eyes widened, and he looked up and around the tent as, over the sounds of panicked people and Brother Nathan's screaming, the deep ethereal sound of a hunting horn rang out.

Silence descended upon the tent like a heavy mist. A pregnant pause, waiting to be filled. Even Brother Nathan's howls seemed subdued as every other soul there held their breath.

The spell broke as the hunting horn sounded out once more. To Lillian, it seemed closer than the previous one. She turned and her eyes met Emily's. The guard who'd been tackling her was already running for the tent flap, ushering out The Eyes. Most of the other occupants had the same idea, and a chokepoint was forming at the entrance.

Brother Nathan's screaming changed to exultant cries. "He has come to avenge us! He has come to lay waste to our enemies!"

Lillian preferred the screaming. "To the back!" Lillian said to Emily and moved towards the rear of the tent. She stopped beside Brother Nathan with his smug smile and welcoming outstretched arms. As he cried, "Destroy our enemies, Lord!", Lillian drove the two-pronged fork up and into his chest cavity, where she judged his heart to be.

Brother Nathan gasped for breath and clutched at the utensil's handle, but his weak grip had no chance of moving it. He dropped to his knees as his heart gave out, then collapsed forward, driving the fork points through his body and out the back a couple of inches.

Lillian continued past the blessedly silent, freshly dead Eye to the back of the tent, shouting, "Emily!"

Emily hadn't moved; she was rooted to the spot. The hunting horn's next call was so loud that Lillian thought she saw the seats on the raised area vibrating. It galvanised Emily into action, and she ran to Lillian's side.

Her eyes were wild, like those of a cornered animal. "What do we do?" There was no need to explain what hearing that horn so close meant.

It means death, thought Lillian. "We use the back door," she said. Emily's confused look at the unbroken canvas turned to understanding as Lillian stabbed into the material with the sharp carving knife and pulled it downwards, creating a jagged exit. She held out the carving knife. "Give me the bow!"

Emily handed Lillian Megan's compound bow and quiver of arrows, and the feel of the familiar weapon in her hands immediately strengthened her. She shouldered the quiver and held the jagged exit open for Emily. "Go!"

Emily stepped through, Lillian on her heels.

———

Outside the tent, the camp was in chaos. To the north, along the road back the way they'd come in, a roiling storm cloud loomed, taking up the horizon. It ended in a thick smog that consumed everything in its wake.

Where they stood, wind swirled around them in gusts, threatening to lift them from their feet. The otherworldly screaming of whatever damned things existed within the dense cloud almost muted the wind's howls.

All around them, the camp's followers rushed back and forth. Some desperately disassembled the tents and packed away equipment, some huddled together in groups as though greater numbers might protect them from the coming storm. The smarter among them took the vehicles and drove south, in the opposite direction from where the storm was coming.

Not that smart, thought Lillian. The storm was moving north to south along the road which passed through the camp. From what Lillian could see, the southern end would become a bottleneck soon because of the panicked escapees. Going north was out of the question; there was no way through the cloud.

Lillian leaned close to Emily and shouted to be heard. "WEST! WE GO WEST!" She gestured to the west in emphasis. As soon as Emily nodded her understanding, Lillian took the lead. Crouching low, as much for additional stability against the wind as to maintain stealth, she moved away from the large tent and into the open. Emily followed close behind.

They made good time until they neared Emily's tent, at which point Lillian felt a hand on her arm and looked down to see that it was Emily. "WHAT?"

"I NEED SOMETHING!" Emily shouted, pointing at the tent.

For fuck's sake, thought Lillian. The storm was too close for comfort for this type of fuckery. "NO!" She shook her head emphatically.

Emily said something Lillian couldn't make out and turned towards the tent. Lillian didn't follow but turned back to look at the camp. Behind her, all movement was more frenetic, with people abandoning their belongings in the face of the impending nightmare cloud. The bottleneck Lillian foresaw had become an actuality, with a trickle of vehicles making it through to the road at a snail's pace. *They won't all make it.*

The hunting horn sounded out again, and it was so loud that Lillian felt it bite at her eardrums and the nerves of her teeth. The screams within scraped the inside of her head. She searched the jacket pockets and found a square of tissue, which she quickly tore in two and rolled into wads, with which she plugged her ears.

Emily had disappeared inside the tent, but Lillian had wasted enough time. She had to crane her neck to see the top of the storm cloud. It was so close, and much wider than she expected. *Enough of this foolishness,* she thought. She turned and resumed her run to the camp's edge, jumping over a latrine pit, the deep intake of its foul odour making her gag. She reached a hedge and slowed to navigate it, squeezing through its tightly interwoven boughs. Then she was free.

To the north, the cloud approached, but she calculated its movement wouldn't come close to her side of the hedge. She backed away just in case. The wind whipped up, and the noise increased, but her improvised earplugs muffled the worst of it. Because of them, she almost didn't hear Emily's screams.

———

Emily got caught on the camp side of the hedge. Without the garish red jacket, Lillian could have easily missed her in the artificial dusk caused by the monstrous cloud.

"Please! Lillian!"

Lillian read the woman's lips more than heard her words. *Fuck!* Every instinct told her to leave Emily where she was. Lillian wasn't to blame for the woman's foolish foray back to her tent. But the woman had saved her life back at the ambush and a debt unpaid when there was a way of repaying it didn't sit well with her. "Fuck!"

She ran back to the hedge, conscious of the cloud bearing down upon them. That close, the screams were a physical thing and when the hunting horn sounded again Lillian thought her heart might give. *I can't take much more of this.*

Emily's eyes were wide and panicked, like livestock about to be slaughtered. Lillian quickly assessed the situation and identified the problem: a stray branch had hooked into a belt loop at the back of Emily's jacket. "Back up!" She pushed her gently to get her moving, but Emily descended into hysterics and fought against the backward movement. She glanced wildly between the looming cloud and Lillian.

We don't have time! With no more room for the soft approach, Lillian shoved Emily backwards. Emily gave her a look of pure terror, but the action produced the desired result and the branch unhooked itself.

The relief on Emily's face was infectious and Lillian smiled at her, but Emily's eyes widened again as her foot caught on something, a root, or stone, and the woman stumbled and fell backwards, landing hard.

"No!" The cloud was only yards away and Lillian saw dark, swirling, twisted shapes and heard the screams of the damned. It drained the heat from her body. "GET UP!"

The proximity of the thick cloud and the shapes within galvanised Emily, and she shot up. She ran through the hedge and almost got to Lillian, but the density of the spot she'd chosen slowed her down again.

"Lillian!"

Emily reached her hand towards Lillian and Lillian grasped it, but at that moment, the cloud rolled over her, obscuring her from Lillian's view.

The hand Lillian gripped grew cold, but Lillian threw herself backwards, using all her weight to pull Emily out. At first nothing happened, and Lillian considered letting go. Already her palm felt an unnatural cold penetrating the skin and her fingers grew numb. Instead, she put everything she had into one last effort and pulled Emily out of the cloud and through the hedge to the other side. Both women landed in a heap as the cloud screamed past them, mere meters away.

CHAPTER 8
RED JACKET

Lillian didn't know how long they lay there while the cloud raged by, and they recovered afterwards. Her breathing was shaky for a long time and when she took the wadded paper from her ears, she could hear similar breathing from Emily.

Finally, she asked, "Emily? Are you okay?"

There was no response. Emily appeared to be sleeping, but when Lillian looked closer, she noticed that the woman's face was covered in a sheen of sweat, yet she felt clammy and cold to the touch. Lillian shook her by the shoulder. "Emily! Wake up!" Then shook her again with more force. "Emily!" The woman moaned incoherently. *Fuck!* Lillian slapped her across the face with enough force that her hand stung.

Emily's eyes flickered, then opened. "Lillian?" she asked in a weak voice. "They wouldn't let me go." She paused, lost in thoughts or memories, and frowned. "Are we dead?"

"We're not dead yet. It was close." Lillian helped Emily sit. "Can you walk?"

Emily nodded, but even that slight movement elicited to swoon.

She looks like death warmed up, thought Lillian. They

couldn't stay there. If there were other survivors, they might return to salvage what they could from the camp. Lillian stood and guided Emily to a standing position, offering what support she could. After a few moments' struggle, Emily swayed beside her, clutching Lillian's arm. "Let's go."

Following the hedge, Lillian half carried Emily down the field until they reached an iron gateway. She helped Emily sit with her back against a tree trunk close to the gate as she ventured into the campsite to see what she could scavenge.

The campsite resembled the level of destruction caused by a hurricane, which Lillian had only ever seen on television. Most of the people were gone without a trace. Only a handful of undead remained, shambling horrors that she gave a wide berth to. After half an hour of searching, she found no usable vehicles. That was her primary goal. Secondary was finding water and food, in that order. She failed with that too and came back to Emily empty-handed. They had Megan's compound bow and some arrows, but Emily had lost the carving knife. Lillian shrugged to herself. *Fuck it.*

Emily looked even more like shit upon Lillian's return, but she was still conscious, so Lillian took that as a win. "Looks like we're walking," she said as Emily lifted her head weakly.

Emily only grunted. Lillian figured she was conserving her energy for something more important than chit-chat. *Staying alive will be hard enough.* Lillian offered her arm and helped the woman up, then supported her as they headed north, in the direction they'd entered the camp the eternity ago that was the previous night.

———

Lillian sagged with exhaustion, even though they were moving at a snail's pace. Based on her estimation, they had covered about half the distance to the farm — a faint trail of smoke persisted, tracing its way into the evening sky as her guiding beacon.

A small cottage stood off the road to the left, and Lillian changed direction towards it. *Maybe there'll be some food, or at least a well.* What she really wanted was a working vehicle, but she wouldn't hold her breath.

The cottage door was open, and she navigated inside with little help from Emily. The woman's condition had clearly worsened since they had set out. Lillian could have abandoned her, but it didn't sit right. She was determined to get help for her, but at the very least, she wouldn't allow her to die alone.

Inside, the cottage had been ransacked like only a place that had been combed through multiple times could achieve. The intruders had stripped most of the suite of furniture in the small lounge, leaving only the skeletal remains of a sofa and two armchairs. The other furniture ended up as kindling. *What the hell were they looking for?*

Lillian sat Emily back against the wall on a section of foam padding. Emily groaned and mumbled incoherently.

Lillian rose and stretched her own back and arms to relieve the tightness. She froze when she heard an approaching engine. Crouching low, she moved to the thankfully grimy window, wiping clear a small spot to peep through.

———

Outside, a Jeep came to a halt opposite the window as Lillian peered through. A slim man in his twenties sat in the passenger seat with his arm hanging outside. Lillian could see the outline of another man further inside the jeep in the driver's seat.

The passenger spoke. "Here'll do. Thanks!"

"Just hurry up," said the driver.

The passenger opened the Jeep's door and hopped out. "Either this or I piss in the cab." He ran to the window where Lillian crouched, unzipped himself, and took out his dick. A moment passed where the passenger sought Zen before the stream of urine began to flow and splash against the wall. The man's face took on a Eureka expression, and he moved the stream up to hose down the window's glass, stripping off a layer of dirt. This seemed to satisfy him.

Lillian watched on with a puzzled look, but she held her breath, so as not to inhale the smell of his urine and to avoid revealing her position through the cleaner glass.

"You think there's anything inside worth looking for, Bren?"

"Quit fucking around, Eoin," said the driver, Bren. He'd gotten out and was stretching his legs on the far side of the vehicle.

"Quit fucking around, Eoin," Eoin mimicked, with a mock stern face.

Lillian almost choked, but pinched herself so she wouldn't guffaw.

Eoin gave the window another splash of piss before shaking himself off. As he walked back to the car, he said, "What's the name of yer one from Star Wars?"

"What?"

Eoin leaned back against the front of the Jeep and lit a cigarette. He inhaled deeply. "The princess. What's was the name of that actress?"

"For fuck's sake," said Bren under his breath, then louder, "The auld one? Princess Leah?"

"Nah. Her Ma, when she was young."

"Natalie Portman? Fucked if I know the character's name..."

"Yeah! That's the one!"

A pregnant silence as Eoin, deep in thought, took another drag of his smoke.

Brendan sighed. To Lillian, it sounded like he'd been through this sort of thing before. "What about her?"

"Remember that film Leon from years ago?"

"The one with the hitman?"

"Yeah, the one with that funny looking French dude."

"Good movie. Is this going anywhere, Eoin?"

Eoin ignored the question. "Yer one, Natalie, was in that too."

"Yep. I remember. So?"

"She was sexy as fuck in that one."

Now it was Brendan's turn for a moment of silence. "You know she was twelve years old in Leon, ya fuckin' pedo."

"Yeah? Well, she's not anymore, so it doesn't count."

"She's probably dead now, but either way, it counts, man." Brendan hopped back into the driver's seat and slammed the door.

"Fuck off!" Eoin wasn't handling Bren's reasoning well, according to Lillian's assessment.

"Just get in the fucking car. We'll find something for you to fuck soon. I can shave all the hair off to make you feel better."

Eoin threw his cigarette on the ground and stamped it out with his boot, before getting back in the Jeep. He stared sullenly straight ahead. "Fuck you, Brendan."

Brendan started the engine, and they pulled away in a cloud of dust.

Lillian breathed a sigh of relief and stood up. She wasn't sure what she just witnessed, but she suspected she'd found the sick bastards she'd been looking for. *Was that only yesterday?* It felt like a week had passed, or an eternity, since she'd been in the ruined church.

From behind her, Emily groaned. The sound caused a sinking sensation in Lillian's stomach. That wasn't the sound of someone with much time left. She rushed to Emily's side and held her hand.

"Lillian?" Emily's voice was barely above a whisper.

"I'm here, Emily," said Lillian. She squeezed the woman's hand.

"It's… so… dark…"

"I'll light us a fire in a minute."

A small shake of Emily's head. She took a shallow breath, exhaled, and that was it.

Lillian squeezed Emily's hand a final time before sitting back against the wall.

"Fuck."

She sat, unmoving, for a while, just resting as she thought of what to do next. Looking at Emily in her provocative clothing and bright red jacket, an idea formed. She quickly searched the cottage for something to bind the woman with and found a few strips of cloth and some electrical cable from the kitchen.

The cloth served as a gag, and Lillian used the cable to bind Emily's hands behind her. Before the first twitches of reanimation occurred, she finished the job. Lillian could safely lead Emily where they needed to go.

Lillian watched from a distance as the small herd, led by a smoker, reached where she'd placed Emily. As soon as the smoker got within ten yards of her, Emily had already turned to follow. She mingled with those already a part of the herd.

Compared to the rest of the undead, Emily stood out like a beacon. It wasn't just the fire engine red patent jacket; Lillian had cleaned her as best she could, too. She looked good. Definitely enough to tempt the assholes who defiled the undead.

She regretted not being able to save Emily but was glad her death would serve some good. *I hope you don't mind, Emily,* she thought. Deep down, Lillian knew that even if the woman minded, it wouldn't stop her from using what she had at hand to achieve her goal.

She had located her vehicle a kilometre from the rundown cottage and had changed out of the ridiculous Biker-girl outfit. She'd gotten some much needed food too, despite memories of the feast in the raider camp causing her stomach to roil. After that, she scoured the area and found the smoker-led herd she'd attached Emily to.

Now I watch and wait. Lillian eagerly anticipated the moment her prey would stumble upon the enticing bait.

THE DARKLE CHRONICLES
BOOK ONE

Shadow Apocalypse

THE DARKLE CHRONICLES
BOOK TWO

Once Upon a Time in Monto

ACKNOWLEDGMENTS

I would like to thank the following individuals for their support and contributions to this project:

Once again, my family, for their patience and understanding when I'm spending time with stories and not with them.

My editors, Jonathan, Hannah, and Candace, who made the invisible, visible, making the final project so much better.

Finally, my readers, for taking the time to read one of my stories for the first time, or for picking up another one. Thanks to all of you. You have my gratitude.

B.C. Hollywood
March, 2024

ABOUT THE AUTHOR

B. C. Hollywood is an Irish author of dark fantasy and extreme horror. He spends much of his spare time battering raw story ideas into shapelier form.

He writes novels, short stories, flash fiction, screenplays, and poetry. He is the author of *Dogcatcher: A Short Story*, the collection *Add me… and other warnings,* and the extreme horror, apocalyptic fantasy series, **The Darkle Chronicles,** of which *Red Jacket* is a prequel to Book One, *Shadow Apocalypse,* and Book Two is *Once Upon a Time in Monto.*

To connect with B.C. and for news of his upcoming titles, check out his website www.bchollywood.com and subscribe to his newsletter.

The third book in **The Darkle Chronicles** series, *The House of Marionettes,* is scheduled for late Summer of 2024 release.